JANE AUSTEN

Children's Stories

Dados Internacionais de Catalogação na Publicação (CIP) de acordo com ISBD

A933p Austen, Jane
Persuasion / Jane Austen. – Jandira : W. Books, 2025.
96 p. ; 12,8cm x 19,8cm. – (Jane Austen Children's Stories)

ISBN: 978-65-5294-182-4

1. Literatura infantojuvenil. 2. Romance. 3. Literatura estrangeira. 4. Literatura inglesa. 5. Amor. 6. Preconceito. 7. Inglaterra. I. Título. II. Série.

2025-594 CDD 028.5
CDU 82-93

Elaborado por Vagner Rodolfo da Silva - CRB-8/9410
Índice para catálogo sistemático:
1. Literatura infantojuvenil 028.5
2. Literatura infantojuvenil 82-93

1st edition in 2025
www.cirandacultural.com.br

JANE AUSTEN

Persuasion

W. Books

Chapter 1

Anne Elliot loved her home at Kellynch Hall. It was a large country house, but its size and grandeur did not matter. Anne loved Kellynch because of all the happy memories she had made there with her mother, who had died many years ago.

Sadly, Anne's task now was to go from room to room, helping the servants to cover up her family's furniture with large sheets.

Since her mother's death, Anne's father and elder sister had spent more money than they had. Now, despite Anne's warnings, the Elliot family could no longer afford to stay at Kellynch Hall. They were going

to rent it out and live somewhere smaller instead.

'We shall go to Bath,' declared Sir Walter Elliot, Anne's father, over one of their final teas at Kellynch. 'I have found a house for us in one of the most fashionable streets in the city.'

'But Father,' interrupted Anne, 'surely we could find somewhere

less expensive than Bath? Perhaps somewhere closer to Kellynch ...'

Anne hated the thought of moving so far away.

'We are going to Bath, Anne!' snapped her elder sister, Elizabeth. 'You don't have to come with us if you don't want to. You can go and stay with Mary.'

Mary was Anne's younger sister. She had married a young man who lived only a few miles away, on an estate called Uppercross. Though her sister meant it as a punishment, Anne agreed that visiting Mary might be a good idea. Only a few days earlier, Mary had written to Anne. It seemed that Mary was suffering from one of her many illnesses.

'In any case,' Elizabeth carried on, nibbling the last slice of sponge cake from the tray, 'I should much rather have Mrs Clay come with us and keep me company.'

It took all of Anne's willpower

to bite her tongue. Mrs Clay was the daughter of the attorney Mr Shepherd, who was helping to find someone to rent Kellynch Hall. Anne disliked the way Mrs Clay always flattered Elizabeth, and the way she fluttered her eyelashes at Anne's father, Sir Walter. If Mrs Clay was going to Bath, then Anne was even more convinced that going to Uppercross was the best thing for her.

On her last morning at Kellynch Hall, Anne looked around the rooms, trying to picture her mother in each one. Reading by the fireplace. Writing letters at her desk. Sitting up in bed to discuss a ball or dinner she had gone to that evening, with Anne snuggled up next to her.

Sir Walter, Elizabeth and Mrs Clay were already in their carriage, ready to leave for Bath.

Anne walked down the front steps of the house to join Mr Shepherd 'Be sure you visit everyone in the village to say goodbye from us,' demanded Elizabeth. 'It's the polite thing to do.'

Of course, Elizabeth wasn't concerned enough about politeness to actually visit the village *herself*.

Anne nodded in agreement and waved goodbye. She was a little ashamed to admit that she was far less saddened to see her father and sister leave than she was to say goodbye to Kellynch Hall.

'Good news, Miss Elliot,' said Mr Shepherd. 'I have found a couple who wish to rent Kellynch Hall.'

Anne smiled. 'I hope they are good people?' she asked.

'Very,' replied Mr Shepherd. He pulled a sheaf of papers from his bag and adjusted his spectacles to read the names. 'An Admiral Croft and his wife. I believe they will be joined by Mrs Croft's brother in due course. Although it doesn't mention his name ...'

'Captain Wentworth,' replied Anne, a little shakily.

'Ah! Do you know him?' asked Mr Shepherd.

'Yes,' replied Anne. 'A little.'

In fact, Anne knew Captain Wentworth very well. Eight years ago, she had even agreed to be his wife.

Chapter 2

Anne remembered little of her journey to Uppercross. Her mind was taken up with memories of Captain Wentworth. Anne had loved him very much, but had been persuaded to break off the engagement by Lady Russell.

Lady Russell had been a great friend of Anne's mother. She had watched over Anne and her

sisters after their mother had passed away. When Lady Russell found out that Anne wanted to marry Captain Wentworth, she was worried. Anne was only nineteen years old at the time, and Captain Wentworth did not have much money to support them.

Anne trusted Lady Russell. After all, if Lady Russell thought the engagement was a bad idea, perhaps her mother would have thought the same way?

And yet, Anne had not met anyone before or since who she had liked even half as much as Captain Wentworth. No one as clever, kind or thoughtful, and no one she could even consider marrying. Eight years on, she still loved Captain Wentworth.

She imagined that he must have married someone else by now, but to hear his name made Anne's cheeks flush and her heart beat hard in her chest. To think that he would soon be living in her old home was thrilling and devastating all at once.

Anne was glad when she finally joined her sister in the parlour of Uppercross Cottage, the little house she shared with her husband, Charles Musgrove, and their two sons. Charles's mother, father and two younger sisters, Henrietta and Louisa, lived in a much bigger house just down the lane that Charles would inherit one day.

‘Oh Anne, at last you are here!’ Mary Musgrove said, blowing her nose with one hand and holding the other out in a greeting.

'How are you, Mary?' Anne said, taking off her cloak.

'Oh, very ill, very ill,' replied Mary with a little cough.

Anne smiled as she removed her bonnet. Mary had been telling people she was ill for the last ten years. Whenever it came to going out for dinner or to a ball, however, she somehow made a miraculous recovery.

She did so that very same day in order to take Anne to see the Musgroves.

Anne always felt very at home when she visited the Musgroves. She enjoyed the company of her brother-in-law and his family very much. Charles was a cheerful man, and his sisters adored Anne. With their help, Anne spent her first week at Uppercross pleasantly. She did very well at not thinking about Captain

Wentworth. Until, that is, one evening at the big house.

'Have you heard the news?' said Henrietta. 'Father has been to visit Admiral Croft at Kellynch.'

'No, no,' interrupted Louisa, giggling. 'The biggest news is that Mrs Croft's brother, Captain Wentworth, was there!'

Anne tried not to blush at the mention of his name.

'He has made his fortune in the navy and is not married,' said Louisa.

'And he's supposed to be terribly handsome!' added Henrietta.

Mrs Musgrove frowned playfully at her daughters. 'My dear Henrietta, it shouldn't trouble you if he were the most handsome man in England. You are already engaged!'

Mary had complained to Anne more than once about Henrietta's engagement to a local man called Charles Hayter. Although Mr Hayter was a nice man, Mary disapproved of him because he was only a farmer.

Anne wished that they would talk about something else. Just then the footman entered the sitting room and announced that Captain Wentworth himself had arrived. Anne stared at the ground as he was shown into the room.

'How lovely to see you again, Captain,' said Mr Musgrove. 'Let me introduce you to my wife, my son, Charles, and his wife, Mary. These are my daughters, Henrietta and Louisa.'

Anne looked up as the introductions came to her.

'And this is Mary's sister, Miss Anne Elliot,' Mr Musgrove added, cheerfully.

Captain Wentworth and Anne looked at each other for a moment. Then Captain Wentworth looked away.

'Miss Elliot and I have met before,' he said in an emotionless voice.

'Yes,' murmured Anne.

Captain Wentworth continued, addressing everyone. 'I have come with a request from my sister. She would like you all to come for dinner this Saturday at Kellynch Hall. You too, Miss Elliot.'

Unable to speak, Anne nodded in reply. Captain Wentworth was invited to stay for a glass of wine, but declined. Anne thought he seemed keen to leave. She breathed more easily once he was gone. That night, alone in her room, she wondered how she was going to make it through a whole evening with him.

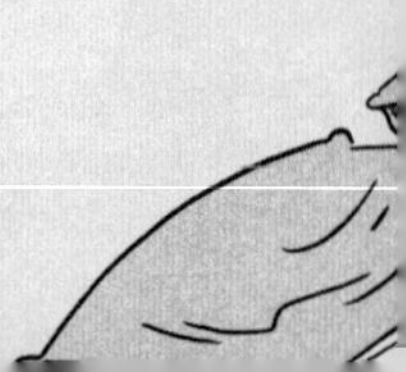

Chapter 3

Mary Musgrove was in a state of panic. Her illness had quite disappeared at the invitation to dine with Admiral Croft at Kellynch Hall. Her only concern on Saturday evening was what to wear. Anne had dressed half an hour ago.

‘Of course, it will be strange to be a guest in the house we grew up in,’ said Mary, trying on two different necklaces. ‘And how on earth do you know Captain Wentworth?’

Anne opened her mouth, but couldn’t find the right words. Suddenly a great deal of shouting could be heard from the garden.

Mary and Charles's eldest son had fallen from a tree. He was in a lot of pain and drifted in and out of consciousness. Charles laid him on the sofa in front of the fire and Anne sent for the doctor. Mary wailed and fanned herself while servants ran to fetch water. The doctor arrived and, with Anne's help, discovered that the boy had dislocated his collarbone. Mary's wailing grew louder.

'Will he be alright?' asked Charles.

'We will need to reset the bone, and he'll need plenty of rest. But yes, he should make a full recovery,' replied the doctor.

'My goodness, what an evening,' Mary said some time later. The doctor had left and she was pacing in front of the fire. 'Anne, you can't know what it is to suffer like I do because you are not a mother.'

Anne said nothing as she placed a cool cloth on the little boy's forehead. Charles began to put on his coat.

'Well, I shall pass on your apologies to Admiral Croft and his wife, my dear,' he said. 'As the little lad is on the mend, I should hurry to Kellynch and put in a late appearance.'

'And why should *you* still go to the dinner while I am left here?' Mary demanded.

'Would you be happy to leave your son when he is unwell?' Charles asked.

'If you are happy to go, then why not I? Simply because I am the mother!'

Anne could not bear the bickering. 'I will stay with my nephew,' she said. 'I do not mind.'

Charles and Mary looked at each other with obvious relief. They could both go to the dinner and not feel guilty for leaving their son. As for Anne, she could avoid an evening of questions about her past with Captain Wentworth.

Chapter 4

The following morning, Mary was so full of stories from the dinner that she almost forgot to ask about the health of her eldest child. Charles was equally delighted at the idea of a morning's hunting with Captain Wentworth. He sat happily cleaning his rifle while his wife wittered away.

'Oh, and Captain Wentworth is so delighted with the girls!' said Mary, buttering a piece of toast. 'I should think he'll have a hard time choosing between them.'

'He doesn't have a choice,' said Charles. 'Henrietta is engaged to Mr Hayter.'

Mary sighed, but didn't start on

her long list of reasons why she disapproved of Mr Hayter.

'I'm afraid Captain Wentworth wasn't very kind about you, Anne,' said Mary, thoughtlessly.

Anne's stomach lurched slightly at the idea of Captain Wentworth discussing her at all.

'He said you had changed so much he barely recognised you,' Mary said.

'I don't think he quite meant it like that ...' Charles began before being cut off by his wife.

'Oh look!' she cried, standing to get a better look out of the dining-room window. 'Here he is now!'

Anne was silent as Captain Wentworth entered the dining room. She knew now that either he was still upset with her for breaking off their engagement, or worse, that he no longer cared.

Had she really changed so much in eight years? Captain Wentworth had perhaps grown older around the eyes, but to Anne he was the same person she had fallen in love with.

Charles was keen to leave and begin hunting, but he was blocked in the hallway by the entrance of his younger sisters.

'We thought we would take Anne for a walk,' said Louisa. 'Captain Wentworth! How lovely to see you again so soon.'

'I know!' cried Henrietta. 'Why don't we all come along on your hunt? We can pay a visit to Mr Hayter on the way.'

So the arrangements were made. Charles and Captain Wentworth would hunt, and Henrietta, Louisa, Anne and Mary would walk alongside.

The path Charles had chosen was perfect for hunting pheasants, but not for ladies out on a morning stroll. They soon came to a muddy little stream, which Charles strode over thanks to a fallen tree. The ladies walked across it with the help of Captain Wentworth, who seemed to forget Anne. Anne swallowed the hurt and tried to cross the tree herself. Halfway across her boots slipped and she ended up ankle-deep in mud, twisting her foot.

At that moment, a hand reached out to help her. Captain Wentworth said nothing as he gently pulled her up and out of the sticky brook.

'Thank you,' Anne said.

'We are here!' Henrietta called from a little farther up the hill. Charles took his sister's arm and accompanied her to the Hayter's farmhouse. Mary refused to join them, using Anne's twisted ankle as an excuse. Louisa and Captain Wentworth said they would take a stroll while Charles and Henrietta paid their visit.

Mary sat heavily on a tree stump and started to complain about Mr Hayter.

Rather than listen, Anne decided that her ankle would feel much better if only she walked on it a little. She set off alone, soon finding herself behind Louisa and Captain Wentworth. She was close enough to hear their conversation.

'Mary has far too much of the

Elliot pride,' Louisa was telling Captain Wentworth. 'I would not care if the man I loved had £50 or £5000. We all wish Charles had married Anne instead . He asked Anne first, you know.'

'And she refused to marry

him?' asked Captain Wentworth.

'Yes,' said Louisa. 'Henrietta and I think she must have a great lost love somewhere whom she cannot forget.'

Anne's face flushed. She wished she could be as far away from that hill as possible, so she turned quietly and returned to Mary.

After everyone had journeyed home together, Captain Wentworth was invited to dine at Uppercross, along with his sister and the Admiral. Anne's heart sank. She did not think she could stand a whole evening of being ignored by Captain Wentworth, or watch as he laughed and danced with Louisa.

Chapter 5

In the end, the dinner at Uppercross was far more enjoyable than Anne had expected. Mr and Mrs Musgrove were as cheerful as ever and Charles made everyone laugh. Mary said very little

and Anne enjoyed the company of the Admiral and his wife, Sophia, a great deal. Sophia had much of the same charm and good-nature as her brother, and her conversation let Anne forget the hurt she had been feeling since the walk.

'I must go to Lyme,' Anne heard Captain Wentworth say. He was talking to Charles, but soon the entire room fell

silent to listen to him.

'My very good friend Captain Harville has moved there recently and I should like to visit him. He was injured the last time we sailed together.'

'We will miss you, Captain,' said Mrs Musgrove.

'I was wondering if perhaps we could make a party and go together,' Captain Wentworth said. 'Lyme is lovely this time of the year.'

Mary clapped her hands together. 'Oh yes!' she said.

And soon it was settled. Mary, Charles, Anne, Louisa and Henrietta would all travel with Captain Wentworth and stay in a hotel near the Harvilles.

On their first day at the seaside, Captain Wentworth introduced his friends to Captain Harville and his wife, as well as another captain who was staying with them: Captain Benwick. Captain Benwick had been engaged to marry Captain Harville's sister, Fanny, that summer. Sadly, Fanny had passed away during their last trip at sea. Captain Benwick was a quiet man, and wore his sadness on his shoulders at all times.

Captain Harville invited the entire party of visitors to stay for dinner. Anne was seated next to Captain Benwick, and she noticed Captain Wentworth watching them from his spot next to Louisa, farther up the table.

'I am sorry to hear of your loss,' Anne said, quietly.

'Thank you,' replied Captain Benwick. 'I loved her very much.'

Anne smiled. 'And what do you like to do, Captain, when you are on leave from the navy?'

'I read. Poetry mostly.'

As Anne was fond of poetry, she began a lengthy discussion with

the sad, young captain. Soon her eyes stopped flicking to Louisa and Captain Wentworth.

The following morning, the group met up again for a walk on the Cobb – a large stone pier that stretched out to sea. Anne lagged behind her sister and the rest of the party to breathe in the sea air.

'You did a good thing last night.' Anne was startled to see that Captain Wentworth had waited for her. 'Benwick hasn't talked so much in months.'

Anne swallowed. 'We talked about poetry,' she said.

Captain Wentworth smiled. 'His favourite subject.'

Anne smiled back. She had forgotten how easy it could be to talk to Captain Wentworth. She was about to speak again when their attention was drawn to the stone steps that spilt the top half of the Cobb from the bottom. Louisa was standing halfway up them.

'Captain Wentworth! Catch me!' Louisa threw out her arms. Captain Wentworth frowned a little, but jogged to the steps to catch and lower Louisa to the bottom. However, Louisa wasn't finished with her game. 'Catch me again!' she cried, and this time she climbed higher.

Various cries of protest came from Charles, Mary and Captain

Wentworth, but Louisa was determined. She leapt from the top step, and this time Captain Wentworth could not catch her. She landed heavily on the stone below.

Chapter 6

Louisa Musgrove was seriously injured by her fall on the Cobb. In the moments after the accident, Anne had taken charge. Pressing Captain Wentworth's neckerchief to Louisa's head wound, she sent someone to find a doctor and ensured that Louisa was taken back to the hotel as soon as possible.

Anne stayed with Louisa through the night, helping the doctor and soothing Henrietta and Mary who took it in turns to weep at Louisa's bedside.

'I think Mr and Mrs Musgrove should be informed,' Captain Wentworth told Charles quietly in the corner of Louisa's room. 'I will take Henrietta home to be with them, and perhaps Mary should come too. Anne is the most capable of any of us. She should stay and look after Louisa.'

Anne continued to wipe the small beads of sweat off Louisa's brow as Mary stood up indignantly. 'Anne? What is Anne to Louisa?' she demanded. 'If anyone should stay, it should be me. I am her sister-in-law.'

Anne could see that Captain Wentworth was readying himself to fight Mary's point. 'I do not mind,' Anne said. 'I will return to Uppercross with Henrietta.'

Anne placed a kiss on Louisa's cheek and headed back to her own room. In the hallway she passed a gentleman in a fine cloak and top hat. He tipped his hat and stared at Anne as she hurried to her room and quickly packed her things.

The journey to Uppercross did not take long. Henrietta was exhausted from crying and slept on Anne's shoulder. It was late when they arrived. Captain Wentworth had to bang on the door for several minutes before a sleepy footman let him in. He broke the news to the Musgroves. Soon Captain Wentworth was ready to ride back to Lyme.

'I must return to see if I can do anything to help,' he said to Anne

'Will you let me know how she is?' Anne asked. 'I shall be joining my family in Bath. Will you write to me there?'

Captain Wentworth nodded. 'Of course.'

They shared a moment of silence together before Captain Wentworth mounted his horse and galloped away into the night.

Chapter 7

Anne did not like Bath. There were too many people. On the day she arrived in Camden Place, Anne found her sister and Mrs Clay chatting secretively in a corner of the parlour. Her father was almost entirely hidden by a newspaper.

'My dear Anne!' Sir Walter said as he lowered his paper. 'We are very glad to see you.'

'What news do you bring from Uppercross?' Elizabeth asked. But before Anne could begin to tell her about Lyme and Louisa, Elizabeth began again. 'Of course, it will be *nothing* to our news …' Elizabeth looked sideways at Sir Walter.

'We have been visited by Mr Elliot,' said Sir Walter, looking rather pleased with himself. 'He is keen for us to be friends.'

Mr Elliot was a distant cousin who, as the next male in line, would inherit Kellynch Hall when Sir Walter passed away. In recent years, Mr Elliot had shown little interest in getting to know the rest of the Elliot family. Clearly that had now changed.

'He has called on us nearly every day,' said Mrs Clay, giggling. 'It seems he has a growing attachment to your family.' She grinned at Elizabeth, who pretended to blush.

Anne smiled politely. If Elizabeth married Mr Elliot it would be very neat and tidy. They may even be able to live at Kellynch Hall again one day.

That afternoon, when Anne had unpacked and was about to set off to see an old school friend who lived in Bath, the footman entered the parlour to announce a visitor.

'Mr Elliot,' the footman boomed. In came the gentleman whom Anne had bumped into at her hotel in Lyme.

'Mr Elliot!' cried Sir Walter. 'How lovely to see you again. May I introduce my younger daughter, Anne.'

Anne smiled at the man, who stared back at her in disbelief. 'Why, I believe we know each other already,' said Mr Elliot.

Elizabeth gave her sister a hard stare. 'You know each other?'

'Well, not really,' said Anne, hearing the jealous tone in her sister's voice. 'I believe we stayed in the same hotel in Lyme.'

Mr Elliot nodded. 'We did. And may I say how wonderful it is to see you again.'

Mr Elliot stayed for just over an hour at the house in Camden Place. He was polite and friendly, and talked to Anne a great deal. But Anne could feel Elizabeth's eyes drilling into her. It was clear Elizabeth wasn't at all happy about the attention he was paying her.

Chapter 8

After Mr Elliot had left, Anne went to visit her old school friend, Mrs Smith. Her husband had died a few years ago and she was now sickly and poor, living in a small house with only her nurse for company. Anne's father and Elizabeth were positively shocked that Anne should want to waste an evening in the company of such a person, instead of going to the Assembly Rooms to gossip.

Anne had no regrets, even before she saw Mrs Smith sitting by her fireplace.

'My dear!' Anne said as she sat beside her. 'It has been too long.'

'It has!' replied Mrs Smith. 'You must tell me everything that has happened to you over the last ten years.'

Anne wondered if she could possibly reveal everything that had happened between herself and Captain

Wentworth. When she tried to find the words, she found that it was too painful. Instead, she talked of her family leaving Kellynch Hall, her trip to Lyme, and finally of meeting Mr Elliot.

At the mention of Mr Elliot's name, Mrs Smith's face fell. 'What is it?' asked Anne.

'I fear Mr Elliot is not a man to be trusted,' Mrs Smith said. 'He knew my husband once, and I'm afraid he was a very bad influence on him.'

Anne nodded. She too had not felt entirely calm in his presence, but he had been so pleasant to her and her family.

‘Perhaps he has improved these past years?’ asked Anne, hopefully.

‘Perhaps,’ said Mrs Smith. ‘But if he has not, Nurse Rook will find out.’ Mrs Smith grinned at the nurse who was gently placing a shawl around her shoulders. ‘Nothing goes on in Bath without her knowing of it!’

The following morning saw the arrival of Lady Russell at the house in Camden Place. Anne was happy to have someone to talk to in the evenings. Her father and Elizabeth always seemed to be in competition over who could spend the most time with Mrs Clay.

Anne decided to take Lady Russell to the Assembly Rooms. She shared everything that had happened in Lyme.

'Poor Louisa!' exclaimed Lady Russell. 'And how is she now?'

'Mary wrote to me a day ago to say she is getting stronger,' Anne replied. 'I expect we shall soon hear of her engagement to Captain Wentworth.'

Lady Russell nodded and looked at Anne. 'And you are … fine with this?'

Anne replied without meeting Lady Russell's eye. 'I am. I must be.'

'And yet you still admire him?' Lady Russell asked. Anne gave no answer. 'Do you blame me for persuading you not to marry him all those years ago?'

'No,' replied Anne, quickly. 'It was my decision to make. It was I who turned him down.'

They walked on in silence for a while before Lady Russell said, 'I believe Mr Elliot has been to visit. Your father tells me he is quite taken with you. What do you think of him?'

Anne was quiet. 'He is perfectly polite,' she replied, and quickly changed the subject.

Chapter 9

There were two letters waiting for Anne as she and Lady Russell returned from the Assembly Rooms. One was a short note from Mr Elliot, thanking Anne for a lovely afternoon the previous day, and expressing his joy that he would be seeing her at

the concert that evening. The second letter was from her sister Mary. Anne felt sure that it would contain news of Louisa's engagement and for a moment she felt like throwing it on the fire. Instead, she excused herself to read the letter alone in her room.

Dearest Anne,

I hope you are now settled in Bath and that my sister and father are well. My illness returned almost as soon as we got back to Uppercross Cottage. I have taken to spending my days on the sofa in the sitting room while Charles takes the boys shooting.

There is, at least, one source of excitement. I refer, of course, to Louisa's upcoming wedding.

Anne stopped pacing her room and sank onto the end of her bed. For a moment she couldn't breathe. Finally, she continued reading.

My mother-in-law and Henrietta have been visiting the best dressmakers in the county. Of course, we were all surprised when Captain Benwick proposed to Louisa . . .

Anne read the line again. Captain *Benwick* had proposed to Louisa? Surely Mary had made a mistake.

. . . however it seemed they became close in Lyme during her recovery. He is a nice fellow, although his fortune isn't as great as Captain Wentworth's, whom we all presumed would propose to Louisa first.

Now Anne's breaths came all too quickly.

So it wasn't a mistake. Captain Benwick was to marry Louisa. Captain Wentworth was unattached.

Anne read the letter again. Her heart was hammering in her chest and she jumped when there came a knock on her door.

Lady Russell took in Anne's flushed face. 'My dear Anne, are you well?'

'Perfectly,' Anne lied.

'Then you had better hurry if you are to change in time for the concert.' Lady Russell smiled, went to Anne's closet and took out an evening dress. 'Mr Elliot will be expecting you.'

Anne nodded politely, but in truth she had quite forgotten about Mr Elliot.

The Assembly Rooms were hot and full of people dressed in their finest. Chatter filled the air as the players tuned their instruments. Anne only half listened as her father, Lady Russell, Elizabeth and Mrs Clay delighted in conversation with Mr Elliot. Then she spotted Captain Wentworth. At first she thought she was seeing things, but it was most certainly him. Captain Wentworth was in Bath.

‘Excuse me,’ Anne said, removing herself from her family and moving quickly through the crowd. She was both surprised and happy when she saw Captain Wentworth’s face break into a wide smile at the sight of her.

‘Miss Elliot,’ he said with a bow.

‘Captain Wentworth, it is good to see you.’

‘It is good to see you, too. I arrived in Bath this morning,’ he replied.

‘How long are you here for?’ Anne asked, wishing their conversation could last all evening.

'I'm not sure,' he replied. He guided Anne to a pair of seats at the back of the concert hall. 'I am staying with Captain Harville who is here to use the famous healing waters for his injury. I am sure he would like to see you.'

Anne was about to take her seat with Captain Wentworth when Mr Elliot suddenly appeared and took her arm. 'Anne, we have saved you a seat in the front row,' he said, ignoring Captain Wentworth.

'Oh, but ...' Anne began.

'Lady Russell insists that you know the music better than any of us,' Mr Elliot continued. 'You should sit with us and hear it better. I am sure this gentleman will not mind.'

Before Anne could introduce Captain Wentworth, and before she could argue any further, Mr Elliot had pulled her away and the concert had begun.

Chapter 10

Anne was furious with Mr Elliot for how rudely he had acted towards Captain Wentworth. At the interval she leapt from her seat to find Captain Wentworth and explain. His chair was empty. He had left the concert, no doubt

cross with Anne for once again being persuaded to do something she did not want to do by her friends and family.

The following morning at Camden Place, Anne was preparing to visit Mrs Smith once more.

'You won't be gone long, will you, my dear?' asked Lady Russell. 'I believe Mr Elliot is going to call. He has something important to discuss with you.'

Anne's stomach sank. If Lady Russell was implying that Mr Elliot was going

to ask Anne to marry him, then she would stay out all day. It was true that by marrying Mr Elliot, Anne would one day be mistress of her beloved childhood home. However, there was only one man Anne could ever see as her husband.

'I am so glad you have come!' Mrs Smith said as Nurse Rook showed

Anne into the little living room. 'I must speak with you about Mr Elliot!'

Anne took off her bonnet. 'What about Mr Elliot?'

Mrs Smith looked at Nurse Rook. 'Nurse Rook has discovered something quite shocking about him,' she began. 'It seems he noticed that Mrs Clay and your father were becoming close.'

Anne nodded. 'Yes, Father seems quite taken with her.'

'Mr Elliot realised that if your father married again and had a son, that he would no longer be in line to inherit Kellynch Hall.'

'I suppose that is true ...' Anne agreed.

'So Mr Elliot has been visiting Mrs Clay in secret, persuading her not to marry Sir Walter, but to be Mr Elliot's mistress, instead.'

Anne was shocked. Surely no one would do such a thing for money? Especially someone like Mr Elliot who was already rich.

'But he is *not* rich,' continued Mrs Smith, when Anne had said this. 'He has debts all over Bath and London. Without your father's money, he will be ruined.'

Anne took a few moments to fully understand what Mrs Smith had told her. She resolved to speak to her father as soon as she got back to Camden Place. He could not marry Mrs Clay when it was clear that she had fallen for the charms of Mr Elliot.

Chapter 11

Instead of heading straight home from Mrs Smith's, Anne took a walk through town to clear her mind. However, she soon found it crowded with thoughts of those precious moments before the concert, when she and Captain Wentworth had spoken so freely with each other. At first she did not hear Captain Harville rushing after her.

'Miss Elliot!' he said, catching up with her at last. 'I am so pleased to see you again.'

'And I you, Captain,' Anne said, smiling.

'I was just on my way to Camden Place to give you this letter from Captain Wentworth.'

Captain Harville passed a letter to Anne. She tried to take it without showing that her hands were trembling.

'Thank you,' said Anne. 'Is Captain Wentworth at home?'

'He went to the Assembly Rooms early this morning,' replied Captain

Harville. 'But he should be on his way back soon.'

Anne forced herself to wait until Captain Harville had left her, before ripping open the seal on the letter.

Anne,

I must speak to you. You pierce my soul. I am half agony, half hope. Tell me that I am not too late, that such precious feelings are not gone forever. I offer myself to you again with a heart even more your own than when you almost broke it eight years ago. I have loved none but you.

Anne pressed the letter to her heart and ran towards the Assembly Rooms. Her feet pounded on the cobbled stones and she ignored the shocked looks

of passers-by. At last, she saw him, chatting to Admiral Croft and his wife, who had just that day arrived in Bath.

'Anne! How lovely to see you!' cried the Admiral. 'You are quite out of breath, are you all right?'

'I am quite well,' replied Anne. She looked at Captain Wentworth and smiled. 'In fact, I believe I am the happiest I have ever been.'

Anne Elliot and Captain Wentworth were married soon after. Although Lady Russell was shocked at first, she accepted the match when she saw how truly happy her young friend was. Sir Walter also approved the marriage, in the face of Captain Wentworth's fortune.

Sir Walter and Elizabeth left Bath, and Mr Elliot disappeared to the countryside after finding out that Anne was engaged to Captain Wentworth. He was joined by Mrs Clay, who seemed as determined to marry him as he was to avoid it.

Louisa and Captain Benwick, and Henrietta and Charles Hayter, had a double wedding at Uppercross. All their friends and family celebrated the day, and Mary didn't complain once of feeling ill.

Anne sometimes wondered what her life would have been like if she

had married Captain Wentworth the first time he had asked her. However, she could not believe that she could have been any happier than she was at that moment. Those eight years had taught her a valuable lesson. She would never be persuaded against her own heart again.